THE CHANGING MAZE

ZILPHA KEATLEY SNYDER

THE CHANGING MAZE

ILLUSTRATED BY
CHARLES MIKOLAYCAK

Aladdin Books
Macmillan Publishing Company   New York
Maxwell Macmillan Canada   Toronto
Maxwell Macmillan International
New York   Oxford   Singapore   Sydney

First Aladdin Books edition 1992
Text copyright © 1985 by Zilpha Keatley Snyder
Illustrations copyright © 1985 by Charles Mikolaycak
All rights reserved. No part of this book may be reproduced or transmitted
in any form or by any means, electronic or mechanical, including
photocopying, recording, or by any information storage and retrieval system,
without permission in writing from the Publisher.
Aladdin Books, Macmillan Publishing Company, 866 Third Avenue,
NY 10022

Maxwell Macmillan Canada, Inc., 1200 Eglinton Avenue East, Suite 200, Don
Mills, Ontario M3C 3N1
Macmillan Publishing Company is part of the Maxwell Communication
Group of Companies.
Printed in the United States of America

10   9   8   7   6   5   4   3   2   1

Library of Congress Cataloging-in-Publication Data
Snyder, Zilpha Keatley.
    The changing maze/ Zilpha Keatley Snyder; illustrated by Charles
Mikolaycak — 1st Aladdin Books ed.
        p.   cm.
    Summary: A shepherd boy braves the evil magic of a wizard's maze to save
his pet lamb.
    ISBN 0-689-71618-4
    [1. Magic—Fiction.   2. Shepherds—Fiction.]   I. Mikolaycak,
Charles, ill.   II. Title.
[PZ7.S68522Cj   1992]
[E]—dc20   91-45323

To Larry–Z.K.S.

To Jesse–C.M.

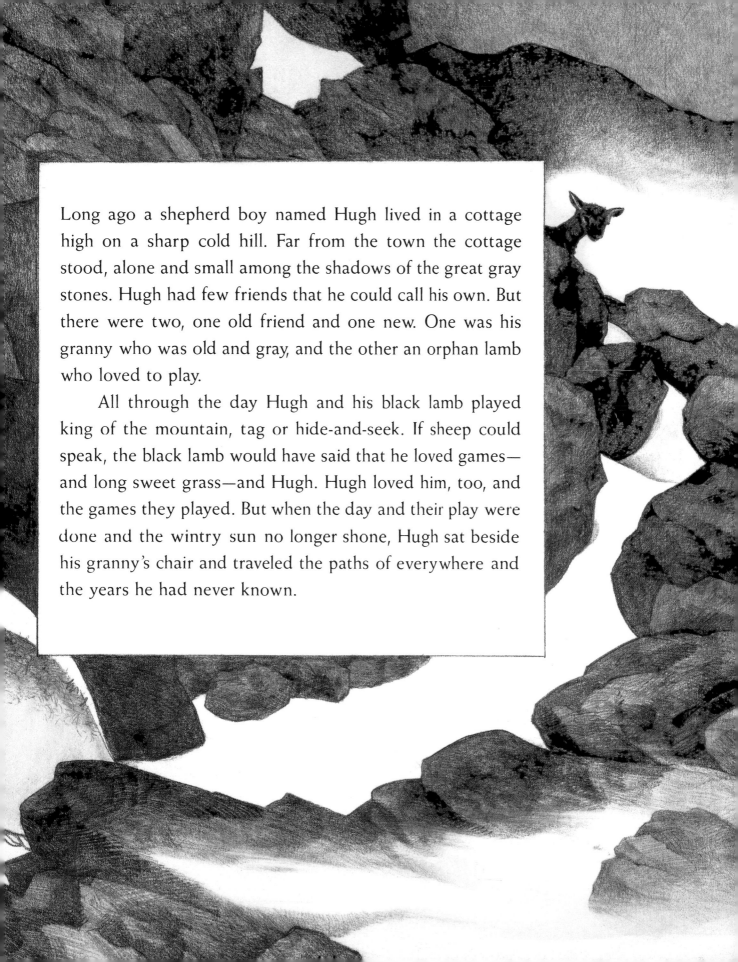

Long ago a shepherd boy named Hugh lived in a cottage
high on a sharp cold hill. Far from the town the cottage
stood, alone and small among the shadows of the great gray
stones. Hugh had few friends that he could call his own. But
there were two, one old friend and one new. One was his
granny who was old and gray, and the other an orphan lamb
who loved to play.

All through the day Hugh and his black lamb played
king of the mountain, tag or hide-and-seek. If sheep could
speak, the black lamb would have said that he loved games—
and long sweet grass—and Hugh. Hugh loved him, too, and
the games they played. But when the day and their play were
done and the wintry sun no longer shone, Hugh sat beside
his granny's chair and traveled the paths of everywhere and
the years he had never known.

Of the many tales that his granny told, there was one that always began the same. "Beware of the Ragged Hills," she'd say, "and the valley that falls from their westward crest. Beware," she'd say, and Hugh knew the rest.

"Long ago," Hugh's granny said, "in the far-off gone-away days, the wizard-king of the Ragged Lands prepared a secret evil plan for a marvelous greenthorn maze. As his gardeners dug and planted and pruned, he watched from a palace tower. And when night fell and the gardeners slept, the wizard-king a vigil kept, and wove his wicked spells.

"The hedge grew thick and wondrous fast, higher and higher, but when at last it towered above the gardeners' heads, they one by one fell deadly ill. So the gardeners died and the secret, too. But the king still knew. And the maze still grew.

'A proclamation then was read in noble homes throughout the land. 'Come one and all,' the message said, 'to see the marvelous greenthorn maze. No maze,' it said, 'has ever been so towering tall, so thorny green. So twisting, curving, turning, bending, crammed with corners and dead endings. So full of mystery—and treasure—for he who solves the riddle it holds can fill his hands with royal gold.'

"And so they came. Grand lords and ladies, royal knights and dames, entered by the narrow iron gate to walk the maze, while, far above, the king looked down from his stony tower with a narrow stony gaze. He watched them wander, blunder, turn and fall, lost in the secret changes of the greenthorn walls.

"Some came out quickly. Some searched for many many days. None of them spoke of what they saw within the maze. But the rumors spread and the whispers grew. *It changes,* the whispers said, *beneath their feet. It changes, even as they seek. The maze changes, and those who seek the gold change, too.* And it was true, for none who walked the king's maze remained the same. Some wept while the world sang. Some stared while the world slept. But each one came and went at the king's call. With hidden hands they came to do his will. And the changing maze was never still.

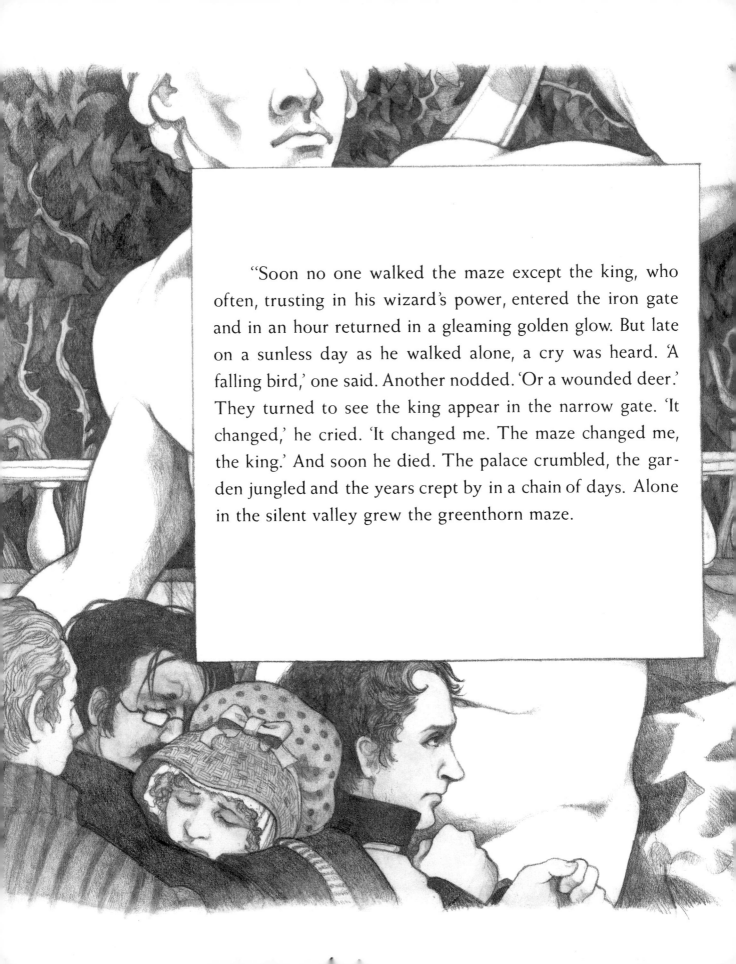

"Soon no one walked the maze except the king, who often, trusting in his wizard's power, entered the iron gate and in an hour returned in a gleaming golden glow. But late on a sunless day as he walked alone, a cry was heard. 'A falling bird,' one said. Another nodded. 'Or a wounded deer.' They turned to see the king appear in the narrow gate. 'It changed,' he cried. 'It changed me. The maze changed me, the king.' And soon he died. The palace crumbled, the garden jungled and the years crept by in a chain of days. Alone in the silent valley grew the greenthorn maze.

"And still, in the deep shadows behind the Ragged Hills, the palace sleeps, and on dark days when lost winds sigh and worry, its gray stones weep." So said Hugh's ancient granny, and he knew that what his granny said was true.

The winter strengthened on Hugh's hillside and the deep snow hid the grass. Hugh's lamb grew lean and restless. And then one freezing day the lamb was gone. On the hillside's snow the tracks were clear and clearly pointed to the west. Hugh followed slowly. All through the Ragged Hills and down into the valley his feet moved on, as if a-gainst his will.

The gray brown grass stood high and tall, there on the
valley floor where no deer dared to graze. No snow fell
here. The air was strangely still. The shepherd's cloak Hugh
wore kept out the cold, but not the chill that widened from
his heart. He saw where the lamb had paused to eat, and
then moved on past the crumbling wall of an ancient tower.
Hugh stopped to call—and heard an answering call.

He hurried then, but he went with dread, through
twisted thickets, under tangled trees, till suddenly above
his head there rose a hedgerow, wide and tall. "The maze,"
Hugh said.

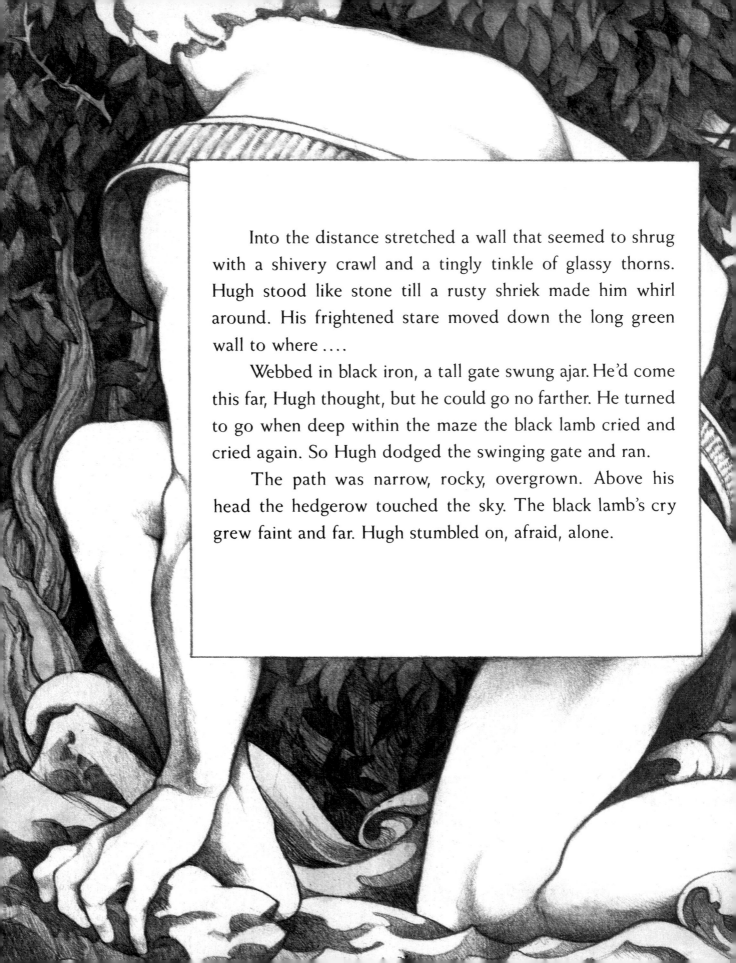

Into the distance stretched a wall that seemed to shrug with a shivery crawl and a tingly tinkle of glassy thorns. Hugh stood like stone till a rusty shriek made him whirl around. His frightened stare moved down the long green wall to where ....

Webbed in black iron, a tall gate swung ajar. He'd come this far, Hugh thought, but he could go no farther. He turned to go when deep within the maze the black lamb cried and cried again. So Hugh dodged the swinging gate and ran.

The path was narrow, rocky, overgrown. Above his head the hedgerow touched the sky. The black lamb's cry grew faint and far. Hugh stumbled on, afraid, alone.

The high walls bent and turned, and as he went he tried to hold them in his mind. He passed a bench, a marble deer, an urn, and stopped to rest. Three turnings more...he passed the urn again. The same one with a rusty crack. He doubled back and walked on fast and tall to hide his fear.

The green walls stretched till near was far, and the lamb's soft cry was almost gone. Hugh ran and walked and walked and ran, turned left, then right, then left again—and stopped before a solid wall that shivered, quivered, turned to haze—and wasn't there at all. So Hugh walked through....

Into a room within the maze—green cliffs around an open space. Hugh heard a bleat, and quickly turned. His lamb was lying at his feet. At first he thought that it was dead, but it opened its eyes when it heard him speak. He knelt and touched its woolly head. "I'll take you home where you belong," he said...but then he heard the song begin.

A sweetly mild and wondrous sound. Hugh raised his head and looked around. An empty room with green grass floor and greenthorn walls—no less, no more, except that now, on a high domed mound, a strange flower bloomed. It glittered golden, hummed a golden song, perfumed the air with promises. Hugh took a long slow breath. The sweet smell breathed and called until ....

His hands outstretched, Hugh climbed the hill.

The flower was gone and in its place, a chest of gold. For a long long time, Hugh looked and looked. His breath came fast, his cold hands shook, as he reached out to take and hold. This was his gold and his alone. And then he heard the black lamb moan.

The small black lamb, Hugh's playful pet, had disappeared again, and yet its cry still lingered in the air—a sudden gasp of pain and fear that Hugh had almost failed to hear, over the lovely golden hum. He found his hands were bent and numb. His legs were stiff. His eyes felt burned, so he closed them tight until he'd turned and stumbled down the grassy hill.

At last Hugh opened his eyes again—and he walked, walked fast, and then he ran. His mind still spun to the golden tune that pulled him back toward the hidden room, except for a secret stubborn part that went on moving his stumbling feet after the sound of the black lamb's bleat.

"It was the lamb who found the gate," Hugh said as he sat beside the grate and fed the fire on a stormy night. His granny's face in the glowing light was wise and warm as she pulled him near. "And the gate," his granny said, "was closed?" He nodded and she nodded, too. "And then," she asked, "what did you do?" "And then," he said, "I put my hand on the black lamb's head and said a prayer and the gate crashed back, and my black lamb and I dashed through."

"I knew," his granny said. "I knew."

The flames burned low in the fireplace, and his granny's eyes were on his face, as if there were more she had to say. She looked at his hands and looked away and tightened her shawl against the cold. "Hugh...if you touch a wizard's gold, it stays forever in your hand, an evil golden wizard-brand."

At first he didn't understand, but then he opened both his hands. "No," he said, "although I tried. And I might have, but the black lamb cried."

His granny smiled and shook her head. "That's why you found your way," she said. "And now the maze will change no more, but always stay just as it is." And that's the way it was—and is—to this very day.

This book was set in fourteen point Weiss.
Typography and binding design by
Charles Mikolaycak and Ellen Friedman.
The drawings were rendered actual size with pencils
and watercolors on a natural vellum paper.

Thanks to Thom, Glenn, Thomas, Phoebe and Carole–C.M.